The children who loved books

For Sophie and Elizabeth,
my favourite storytellers

First published in the UK in 2017
by New Frontier Publishing (Europe) Pty. Ltd.
93 Harbord Street, London SW6 6PN
www.newfrontierpublishing.co.uk

ISBN: 978-1-912076-52-9

A CIP catalogue record for this book is available from the British Library.

Printed in China
10 9 8 7 6 5 4 3 2 1

The children who loved books

PETER CARNAVAS

NEW FRONTIER PUBLISHING

Angus and Lucy didn't have very much.

They didn't have a television.

They didn't have a car.

They didn't even have a house.

But Angus and Lucy had books ...

hundreds of them.

They were stacked here

and piled there,

balanced, propped and shoved
in all kinds of odd places.

Books cluttered every corner of their home,

until one day ...

their home could take no more.

The books had to go.

But things were not the same.

Bowls slid off the table.

Angus couldn't reach the window.

And because there was more space in their home,

there was a lot more space between them all.

Then one afternoon,
something tumbled from Lucy's schoolbag.

'What's this?' said Dad.
'A book,' Lucy answered.
'From where?' asked Mum.
'The library,' Lucy replied.

Mum and Dad looked at the book. They opened it.
Dad read the first sentence aloud, then the second.

The children moved closer
as Dad turned the page and read on.

The light faded and the family moved inside,
Dad reading all the way.

They huddled beside the lamp
and listened to the story.

That night, as darkness fell upon the town,

one small home shone brighter than any other.

The next day, as the family yawned their good mornings, they were closer than ever before.

With bleary eyes and full hearts,
they rode through the clean morning air.

Nobody had said a word, but
Angus and Lucy knew exactly where they were going.

Angus and Lucy didn't have very much,
but they had all they would ever need.